For M and M

First US edition 2021
First published by Templar Books, an imprint of Bonnier Books UK, 2019

Library of Congress Catalog Card Number pending
ISBN 978-1-5362-1704-9

21 22 23 24 25 26 TLF 10 9 8 7 6 5 4 3 2 1

Printed in Dongguan, Guangdong, China

This book was typeset in Times New Roman.
The illustrations were done in ink and watercolor.

TEMPLAR BOOKS
an imprint of
Candlewick Press
99 Dover Street
Somerville, Massachusetts 02144

www.candlewick.com

Sam Usher

FREE

t

templar books

an imprint of Candlewick Press

When I woke up
this morning,
one of the birds
was sick.

I said, "Granddad,
we have to do something!"

So we made him a cozy bed and
Granddad found his book of bird facts.

We gave him some water and Granddad said,
"Look! He's getting better already.
Let's put him back outside."

I said, "Do we have to?"

And Granddad said,
"Yes, I think so.
He won't want to be
cooped up in here."

So we put him
back outside
and thought,
That's that.

It was time for breakfast, so we got some flour,

added milk and eggs, then whisked it all up . . .

and made pancakes.

And I said, "Granddad!
Look who it is!"

"Maybe he's hungry.
Can we give him some of our pancakes?"

And Granddad said, "Let's see if he likes
berries instead."

So we put him by
the blackberry bush
and thought,
That's that.

When it was time for lunch,
we sliced some bread,

got out the fillings . . .

and made triple-deckers.

And I said, "Granddad! Look who it is!"

"Do you think he might be lonely?"

And Granddad said, "He might be. Let's take him outside
in case any of his friends show up."

So we put him
by the birdbath
and thought,
That's that.

In the afternoon, we chose
our favorite cups,

boiled some water,

filled the teapot . . .

and got out the cookies.

And I said, "Granddad!
Look who it is!
I think he likes us.
He keeps coming back."

We spent the rest of the afternoon together.

And I said,
"Granddad, please can he stay forever?"

But Granddad said,
"I think he'll be happier if he's free.
We need to find a tree like this one and
help him find his way home."

So we gathered our expedition equipment . . .

and I said, "Look, Granddad, there's the tree, right at the top of that mountain!"

It was a long
way away . . .

but we made it!

When Bird's
friends arrived . . .

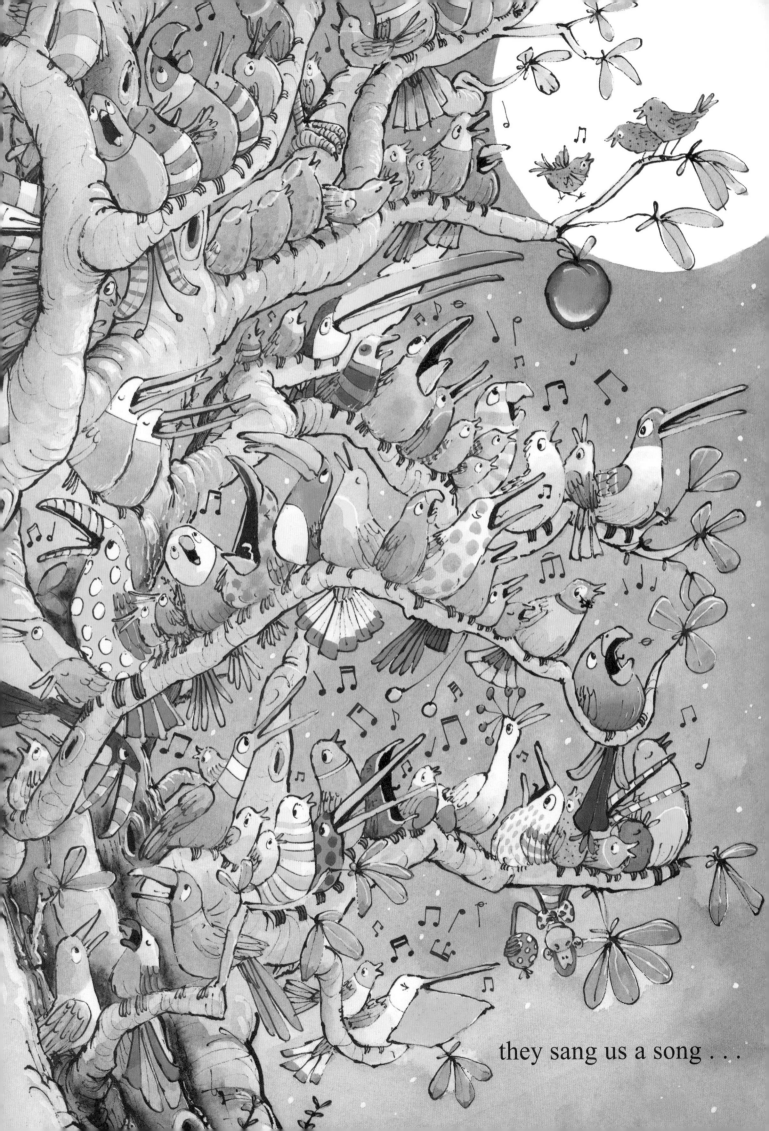

they sang us a song . . .

and shared their midnight feast.

Then they
flew us all the
way home!

And we were back
in time for breakfast.

Granddad said,
"Our little bird
will be happy now
that he's with all
his friends."
And I agreed.

But I hope he visits
again tomorrow.